Dear Parent:
Your child's love of reading starts here!

Every child learns to read in a different way and at his or her own speed. Some go back and forth between reading levels and read favorite books again and again. Others read through each level in order. You can help your young reader improve and become more confident by encouraging his or her own interests and abilities. From books your child reads with you to the first books he or she reads alone, there are I Can Read Books for every stage of reading:

SHARED READING
Basic language, word repetition, and whimsical illustrations, ideal for sharing with your emergent reader

BEGINNING READING
Short sentences, familiar words, and simple concepts for children eager to read on their own

READING WITH HELP
Engaging stories, longer sentences, and language play for developing readers

READING ALONE
Complex plots, challenging vocabulary, and high-interest topics for the independent reader

ADVANCED READING
Short paragraphs, chapters, and exciting themes for the perfect bridge to chapter books

I Can Read Books have introduced children to the joy of reading since 1957. Featuring award-winning authors and illustrators and a fabulous cast of beloved characters, I Can Read Books set the standard for beginning readers.

A lifetime of discovery begins with the magical words "I Can Read!"

Visit www.icanread.com for information
on enriching your child's reading experience.

Rio

LEARNING to FLY

Rio: Learning to Fly
Rio © 2010 by Twentieth Century Fox Film Corporation. All Rights Reserved.
Printed in the United States of America.
No part of this book may be used or reproduced in any manner whatsoever without written permission except in the case of
brief quotations embodied in critical articles and reviews. For information address HarperCollins Children's Books, a division of
HarperCollins Publishers, 10 East 53rd Street, New York, NY 10022.
www.icanread.com
Library of Congress catalog card number: 2010941625
ISBN 978-0-06-201488-7

Typography by Rick Farley

11 12 13 14 15 LP/WOR 10 9 8 7 6 5 4 3 2 1   ❖   First Edition

I Can Read!

READING 2 WITH HELP

RiO

LeaRNiNG to FLY

Adapted by Catherine Hapka
Based on the motion picture screenplay
by Todd R. Jones and Earl Richey Jones

HARPER
An Imprint of HarperCollinsPublishers

BLU

Blu is one of the last blue Spix's Macaws.

He is afraid to fly.

JEWEL

Jewel also is a blue Spix's Macaw.

Before she met Blu, she lived in the jungle.

LINDA

Linda is Blu's owner and his best friend.

RAFAEL

Rafael is a fun-loving toucan.

He loves to sing and dance.

Blu is a rare blue Spix's Macaw
who lives in Moose Lake, Minnesota.
Linda owns Blue Macaw Books.
She and Blu are best friends.

Blu was happy living with Linda.

He learned to climb

and ride a skateboard to get around.

Who cared about flying?

Not Blu!

Still, sometimes Blu saw other birds
flying around outside.

He couldn't help wondering
what it would be like to fly.

But every time he tried,

he either got scared

or he crashed to the ground.

Blu was pretty sure

he just wasn't meant to fly.

One day a scientist named Tulio

showed up at Linda's store.

He told her that Blu

was the last male of his kind.

He convinced Linda to take Blu to

Rio in Brazil.

In Rio, Tulio introduced Blu to Jewel.

Jewel was the last female blue Spix's Macaw.

But Jewel didn't care about meeting Blu.

She just wanted to escape

from Tulio's conservation center.

Before Jewel could break out,
someone birdnapped her and Blu.
They were taken to a warehouse.
Jewel tried to escape.

But when Jewel took off

Blu didn't follow her.

Jewel didn't understand

why Blu didn't fly away.

Jewel thought all birds could fly.

She never imagined that Blu couldn't.

The smuggler that caught Blu and Jewel
chained them together.
After the smugglers left,
Blu unlatched the cage door.

"Let's fly!" Jewel said.

Finally Blu had to admit the truth.

"I can't," he told her.

Since she was chained to Blu,
Jewel couldn't fly now, either.
They had to jump and run
to get away from the bad guys.

Together, Blu and Jewel escaped.

Jewel wished they could fly up

to the safety of the treetops.

Blu wanted to find Linda

and go home to Moose Lake.

The next day Blu and Jewel

tried to find someone to help them

get the chain off their legs.

They met a toucan named Rafael

who said he knew everyone in Rio.

Rafael had a friend who could help.

But he was very far away.

So Rafael decided it was time

for Blu to learn how to fly.

Rafael took Blu and Jewel

to the top of a cliff.

Blu looked down and said,

"I don't think this a good idea."

"Flying isn't what you
think in your head," Rafael said.
"It's what you feel in your heart."

Blu was terrified as he and Jewel
ran toward the edge of the cliff.
"Come on, Blu!" Jewel said.
She took off—but Blu didn't!

"Oh no, not again!" Jewel cried.

She and Blu tumbled down

and landed on top of a hang glider!

At first, Blu was glad to be alive.

Then he looked around

as they soared through the air.

"Wow, this is incredible!" he cried.

Finally Blu knew what it was like to fly.

"See what you've been missing?"

Jewel asked Blu.

"Yes!" Blu cried.

"I feel it!"

He spread his wings—

and tipped right off the glider!

He and Jewel tumbled down

and hit a hang-glider pilot.

They all screamed.

The glider crashed on the beach.

Luckily, everyone was okay.

And now they were a little closer

to finding Rafael's friend.

Blu and Jewel thought

Rafael's friend would be a bird.

He wasn't.

He was a scary, slobbery bulldog

named Luiz.

But Luiz turned out to be very nice.

He knew how to

help free Blu and Jewel.

But even after the chain was off,

Blu still couldn't fly.

If Blu is going to find Linda,

he will have to conquer his fears.

He has to learn to fly

if he's ever going to be able

to follow his heart.